AF575542

# Tennessee Walking Horse

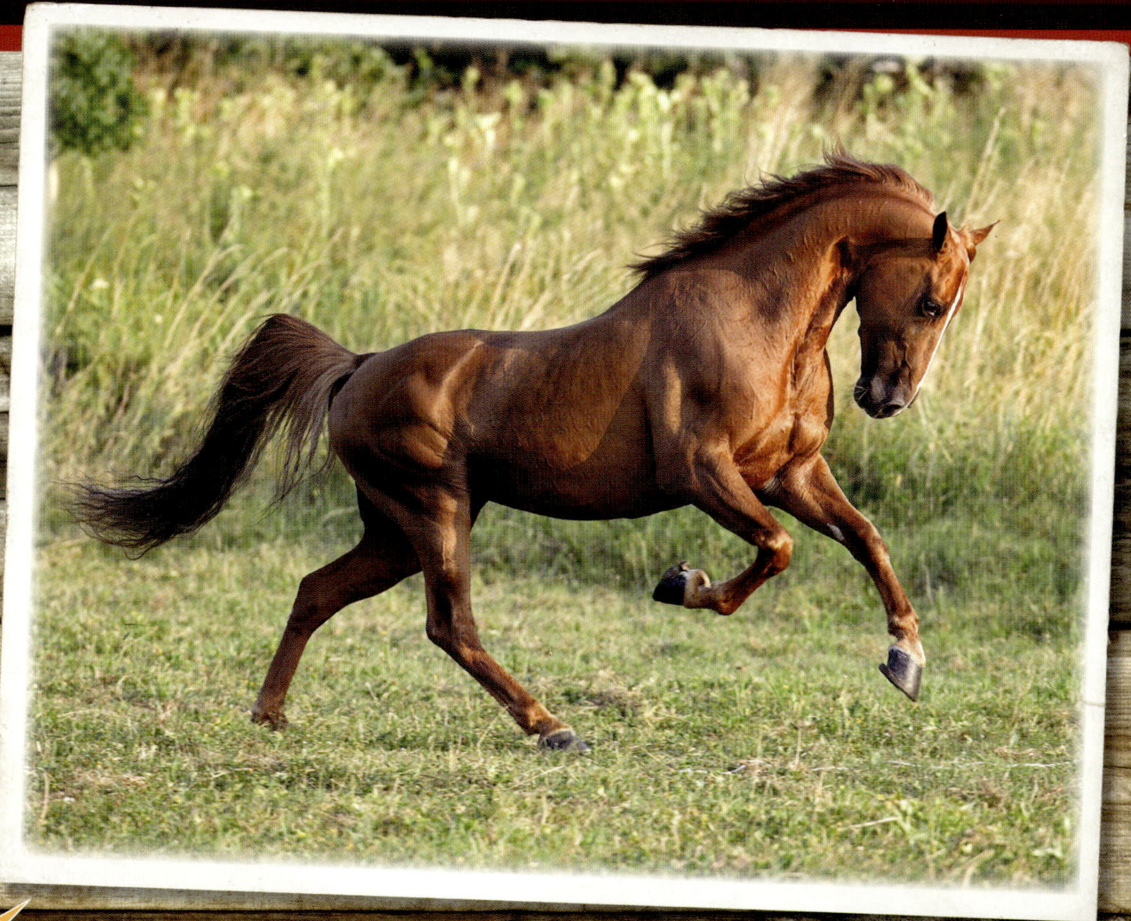

EZ READERS

Marylou Morano Kjelle

## Creating Young Nonfiction Readers

*EZ Readers* lets children delve into nonfiction at beginning reading levels. Young readers are introduced to new concepts, facts, ideas, and vocabulary.

## Tips for Reading Nonfiction with Beginning Readers

**Talk about Nonfiction**

Begin by explaining that nonfiction books give us information that is true. The book will be organized around a specific topic or idea, and we may learn new facts through reading.

**Look at the Parts**

Most nonfiction books have helpful features. Our *EZ Readers* include a Contents page, an Index, and color photographs. Share the purpose of these features with your reader.

**Contents**

Located at the front of a book, the Contents displays a list of the big ideas within the book and where to find them.

**Index**

An Index is an alphabetical list of topics and the page numbers where they are found.

**Photos/Charts**

A lot of information can be found by "reading" the charts and photos found within nonfiction text. Help your reader learn more about the different ways information can be displayed.

With a little help and guidance about reading nonfiction, you can feel good about introducing a young reader to the world of *EZ Readers* nonfiction books.

Mitchell Lane
PUBLISHERS

2001 SW 31st Avenue
Hallandale, FL 33009
www.mitchelllane.com



First Edition, 2021.

Author: Marylou Morano Kjelle
Designer: Ed Morgan
Editor: Morgan Brody

Names/credits:
Title: Tennessee Walking Horse / by Marylou Morano Kjelle
Description: Hallandale, FL :
Mitchell Lane Publishers, [2021]

Series: Popular Horse Breeds
Library bound ISBN: 978-1-68020-573-2
eBook ISBN: 978-1-68020-574-9

EZ readers is an imprint of Mitchell Lane Publishers.

Photo credits: Freepik.com, Shutterstock

# CONTENTS



Words in **bold** can be found in the Glossary.

Tennessee Walking Horses are also called Tennessee Walkers.

## Did You Know?

The Tennessee Walking Horse is the **official** horse of the state of Tennessee.

They have a long **sloping** shoulder and hip. Their back is short. Their eyes are large. Their ears are short. They have a long neck.

## DID YOU KNOW?

Many Tennessee Walking Horses are used in parades and some specifically in the Indy 500 and the Super Bowl.

Their **coat** can be black, brown, gray, yellow, or pure white.

Walkers weigh between 900–1,200 pounds (408–544 kg). They are about 15–17 **hands** tall.

They eat grass, hay, oats, and corn. It takes about 330 days (11 months) for a Walker **foal** to be born.

They have a special way of walking. It is called the running walk.

## Did You Know?

The Tennessee Walking Horse inherits the running walk **gait**. No other breed of horse does it. It can't be taught to another breed of horse.

They nod their head and click their teeth in time to their steps.

## Did You Know?

Because of its smooth gait, the Tennessee Walker is often called the "rocking horse."

They travel between 6–12 miles (10–29 km) per hour.

## DID YOU KNOW?

The Tennessee Walking Horse has many other horse breeds in its **pedigree**. Some are the Narragansett Pacer, Standardbred, and Morgan.

Tennessee Walking Horses are gentle horses.

# GLOSSARY

**coat**
The hair covering the body of an animal

**foal**
A baby horse

**gait**
The way a person or an animal walks

**hand**
A unit of measure equal to 4 inches, used to measure the height of a horse

**official**
Approved by a government

**pedigree**
Family tree, family history, family background, genetic makeup

**sloping**
Slanted

# Sources


Blocksdorf, Katherine. "Meet the Tennessee Walking Horse." *The Spruce Pets*. https://www.thesprucepets.com/meet-the-tennessee-walking-horse-1885862. Retrieved 30 July 2019.

"Breeds of Livestock - Tennessee Walking Horse." *Oklahoma State University*. http://afs.okstate.edu/breeds/horses/tennesseewalking/index.html/. (Retrieved 30 July 2019).

Draper, Judith. *The Complete Horse Book: The Ultimate Guide to Horse Breeds and a Practical Horse Care Manual*. London: Anness Publishing Limited, 1996.

Dutson, Judith. *96 Horse Breeds of North America*. North Adams, MA: Storey Publishers, 2005.

Edwards, Elwyn Hartley. *Eyewitness Handbook: Horses*. New York: Dorling Kindersley, 1993.

"Mare Gestation Calculator." *The Horse*. Thehorse.com. Retrieved 18 September 2019.

"State Symbols." *Tennessee State Government*. https://www.tn.gov/about-tn/state-symbols.html (Retrieved 30 July 2019).

"Tennessee Walking Horse." *Knowledge Based Look-See*. http://knowledgebase.lookseek.com/Tennessee-Walking-Horse.html (Retrieved 30 July 2019).


# Further Reading

### Web Pages

Layos, Allie. "Everything You Need to Know About the Tennessee Walking Horse." *Wide Open Pets*. https://www.wideopenpets.com/all-you-need-to-know-about-the-tennessee-walking-horse/

"The Tennessee Walking Horse." *Gaited Horses*. http://www.gaitedhorses.net/BreedArticles/twhfacts.htm

The Tennessee Walking Horse Association. https://www.twhbea.com/

### Books

Crisp, Marty. *Everything Horse: What Kids Really Want to Know about Horses* (Kids FAQS). New York: Cooper Square Publishing LLC., 2005.

Edwards, Elwyn Hartley. *The Horse Encyclopedia*. London: DK, 2016.

Green, Sara. *The Tennessee Walking Horse*. Hopkins, MN: Bellwether Media, 2011.

*Horses: The Definitive Catalog of Horse and Pony Breeds*. New York: Scholastic Inc., 2019.

# Index



# About the Author

**Marylou Morano Kjelle** lives and writes in Central New Jersey. She is a retired college English professor and the author of over 50 books on various topics for children and young adults. She learned a lot about the Tennessee Walking Horse while researching and writing this book. Marylou especially enjoyed learning how this breed's calm nature makes it a good horse to star in movies and television shows.